Dear Parent:

Congratulations! Your child is taking the first steps on an exciting journey. The destination? Independent reading!

STEP INTO READING® will help your child get there. The program offers five steps to reading success. Each step includes fun stories and colorful art. There are also Step into Reading Sticker Books, Step into Reading Math Readers, Step into Reading Phonics Readers, Step into Reading Write-In Readers, and Step into Reading Phonics Boxed Sets—a complete literacy program with something for every child.

Learning to Read, Step by Step!

Ready to Read   Preschool–Kindergarten
• big type and easy words • rhyme and rhythm • picture clues
For children who know the alphabet and are eager to begin reading.

Reading with Help   Preschool–Grade 1
• basic vocabulary • short sentences • simple stories
For children who recognize familiar words and sound out new words with help.

Reading on Your Own   Grades 1–3
• engaging characters • easy-to-follow plots • popular topics
For children who are ready to read on their own.

Reading Paragraphs   Grades 2–3
• challenging vocabulary • short paragraphs • exciting stories
For newly independent readers who read simple sentences with confidence.

Ready for Chapters   Grades 2–4
• chapters • longer paragraphs • full-color art
For children who want to take the plunge into chapter books but still like colorful pictures.

STEP INTO READING® is designed to give every child a successful reading experience. The grade levels are only guides. Children can progress through the steps at their own speed, developing confidence in their reading, no matter what their grade.

Remember, a lifetime love of reading starts with a single step!

To Erik, the wind beneath
my wings —S.A.

Copyright © 2013 Disney Enterprises, Inc. All rights reserved. Published in the United States by Random House Children's Books, a division of Random House, Inc., 1745 Broadway, New York, NY 10019, and in Canada by Random House of Canada Limited, Toronto, in conjunction with Disney Enterprises, Inc.

Step into Reading, Random House, and the Random House colophon are registered trademarks of Random House, Inc.

Visit us on the Web!
StepIntoReading.com
randomhouse.com/kids

Educators and librarians, for a variety of teaching tools, visit us at
RHTeachersLibrarians.com

ISBN 978-0-7364-3018-0 (trade) — ISBN 978-0-7364-8119-9 (lib. bdg.)

Printed in the United States of America   10 9 8

STEP INTO READING®

STEP 2

Disney
PLANES

DUSTY FLIES HIGH

By Susan Amerikaner

Illustrated by the Disney Storybook Artists

Random House 🏠 New York

Dusty is
a crop-dusting plane.
He dreams of being
a great racer!

Dusty's friend Chug
helps him from below.

Dottie fixes planes.

She tells Dusty,

"You're not meant to race."

Dusty tries out
for the big race anyway.

Dusty flies fast through the turns.

<u>ZOOM!</u>

He does well.

Dusty will fly in the
around-the-world race.
His friends are
very proud of him.

The race begins!
Dusty tries to fly high.
But flying high
makes him feel sick.

Dusty flies low.
He almost hits
an iceberg.
<u>BRRR!</u>

Another plane
has trouble, too.
He gets oil in his eyes.
He cannot see!

Dusty slows down.
He helps the plane
land safely.

Dusty's crop-dusting gear
is heavy.
He takes it off
and flies faster.
He is a fan favorite!

One plane is not a fan.

His name is Ripslinger.

He wants to be

the only winner.

Dusty flies fast and low through a tunnel.

Look out, Dusty!

Here comes a train!

Dusty keeps flying
faster and faster.
He is soon
in first place.

Ripslinger is mad.

Ripslinger's friend
breaks Dusty's antenna.

Dusty gets lost
over the ocean.

Dusty lands on a ship.
The jets and pitties
fix and refuel him.

Dusty gets back
in the race.
He still flies low.

Dusty flies into a storm.

He crashes
into the ocean.

A helicopter pulls Dusty
out of the water.

In the medical hangar,
Dusty is safe.
But he is sad.

Dusty cannot finish
the race.
His parts are broken.
Dottie cannot fix them.

The other racers
visit Dusty.
They share their parts
with him.

Dottie fixes Dusty fast.

He is back in the race!

Dusty flies high,
way up in the clouds.
He flies faster than ever.

Dusty passes Ripslinger.

Dusty wins the race!

Dusty's friends cheer!
His dream has come true.
Dusty has become
a great racer!